Not Smart Enough?

"You don't think I'm smart, but I am!" Jessica shouted. "I studied all week, and I know a lot of very hard words! Maybe I'll even win the spelling bee."

Elizabeth felt awful. She hated to see Jessica sad and angry.

"Prove it," Lila said. "Can you spell *carbohydrate*?"

"Um . . . C-A-R-B-O—" Jessica stopped in the middle of the word. Her face was getting pinker and pinker.

"Can you spell the rest?" Winston asked nervously.

Jessica looked like she was about to cry. "I hate you all!" she cried out. She turned and ran back inside.

Bantam Skylark Books in the
  SWEET VALLEY KIDS series
Ask your bookseller for the
  books you have missed

SWEET VALLEY KIDS
SUPER SNOOPER EDITION

SWEET VALLEY KIDS

JESSICA AND THE SPELLING-BEE SURPRISE

Written by
Molly Mia Stewart

Created by
FRANCINE PASCAL

Illustrated by
Ying-Hwa Hu

A BANTAM SKYLARK BOOK®
NEW YORK · TORONTO · LONDON · SYDNEY · AUCKLAND

RL 2, 005–008

JESSICA AND THE SPELLING-BEE SURPRISE
A Bantam Skylark Book / August 1991

Sweet Valley High® *and Sweet Valley Kids are registered trademarks of*
Francine Pascal

Conceived by Francine Pascal

Produced by Daniel Weiss Associates, Inc.
33 West 17th Street
New York, NY 10011

Cover art by Susan Tang

ISBN 0-553-15917-8

Published simultaneously in the United States and Canada

Bantam Books are published by Bantam Books, a division of Bantam
Doubleday Dell Publishing Group, Inc. Its trademark, consisting of the
words "Bantam Books" and the portrayal of a rooster, is Registered in U.S.
Patent and Trademark Office and in other countries. Marca Registrada.
Bantam Books, 666 Fifth Avenue, New York, New York 10103.

PRINTED IN THE UNITED STATES OF AMERICA

CWO   0 9 8 7 6 5 4 3 2 1

To Joshua Ross Weinstein

CHAPTER 1

May the Best Speller Win

Elizabeth Wakefield hurried into her second-grade classroom and put down her books. She had something to ask her teacher, Mrs. Otis.

"Is the spelling bee today?" she asked.

"Yes, it is, Elizabeth," Mrs. Otis said with a smile. "I hope everyone will enjoy it."

"Not me," said Jessica, Elizabeth's twin sister. "I'm going to hate it."

Elizabeth turned around. "Come on, Jessica. It'll be fun."

"Spelling is not fun," Jessica said as she

walked to the teacher's desk. "Anyway, I'd never win."

"That's not true, Jessica," Mrs. Otis said. "You're a fine speller when you try. And if you concentrate today, you just might surprise yourself."

Jessica frowned. "Elizabeth is much smarter," she said.

"That's silly," Elizabeth said.

"Yes, it is," Mrs. Otis agreed. "You're both smart. Now take your seats. And, Jessica, think about what I said."

It was true that Elizabeth got better grades than Jessica, but that was only because Elizabeth liked school and worked hard. She enjoyed doing homework, and she loved reading books. She also loved playing soccer and had recently joined the Sweet Valley Soccer League.

Jessica disliked school. She thought the best part of the day was recess. She had trouble settling down during class and often giggled with her friends. She didn't like soccer. In fact, Jessica had not even tried out for the league. She preferred playing with her dolls and doing other things that didn't get her clothes dirty.

Some people were surprised that Jessica and Elizabeth had different likes and dislikes, because they looked exactly the same. Both girls had blue-green eyes and long blond hair with bangs. Each of them wore a name bracelet, too. That made it easier for their friends to tell them apart, especially when they wore identical outfits to school.

No matter how different they were, though, Jessica and Elizabeth were best friends. They shared a bedroom and sat side by side in class.

Mrs. Otis finished taking attendance. "It's time to go to the auditorium," she announced. "The second-grade classes will be the first ones to compete."

The class walked two by two to the auditorium. It was filled with second-graders.

"Everyone please line up on the stage," called out Mrs. Armstrong, the principal.

Elizabeth was nervous, but she was excited, too. Spelling was one of her best subjects.

The principal explained what happens in a spelling bee. Each student would walk to the front of the stage. Then, Mrs. Armstrong would pronounce the word. The student had to say the word, then spell it, then say it

4

again. If the word was spelled correctly, the student stayed up on stage. If the word was spelled incorrectly, the student had to go sit down in the audience.

Everyone scrambled onto the stage.

Kids were pushing and whispering. Elizabeth held Jessica's hand tight. They stood near the front of the line.

"First contestant, please," Mrs. Armstrong said.

Andy Franklin stepped to the front of the stage.

"The word is *yak*," Mrs. Armstrong said.

"*Yak*," Andy repeated loudly. "Y-A-K. *Yak*."

"Good, Andy," Mrs. Armstrong said. "Go to the end of the line and wait for your next turn."

"That was simple," Jessica whispered to Elizabeth.

Three more students had turns. Then Elizabeth reached the front of the line. Her word was *banana*. "B-A-N-A-N-A," she spelled. When she went to the end of the line, she gave Jessica a good-luck wave.

"The word is *frown*," Mrs. Armstrong told Jessica.

Jessica frowned and looked back at Elizabeth. Elizabeth crossed her fingers behind her back.

"*Frown*. F-R-O-W-N. *Frown*." Jessica said quickly.

"Very good, Jessica," said Mrs. Armstrong.

Several people after Jessica missed their words and went to sit down in the audience. Soon, Jessica and Elizabeth were up again. Elizabeth had to spell *gerbil* and Jessica had to spell *dinosaur*. They both got their words right.

After six turns, Elizabeth and Jessica were left with three other second graders. "You're doing great," Elizabeth whispered to Jessica.

"It's just luck," Jessica said. "I'm getting all the easy words."

Elizabeth didn't think it was luck. She thought Jessica was smart.

In the next round, two kids were eliminated. Only Elizabeth, Jessica, and Bobby Amado, who was from Mr. Fein's class, were left.

"*Gorilla*," said Mrs. Armstrong.

Bobby cleared his throat. "*Gorilla*. G-E-R-I-L-L-A. *Gorilla*."

"I'm sorry, that's incorrect," said the principal. "Next."

Elizabeth stepped forward. She had to spell gorilla, since Bobby had missed it.

8

"*Gorilla*. G-O-R-I-L-A. *Gorilla*," she said carefully.

"No, I'm sorry, that's incorrect, too. Next."

Elizabeth felt disappointed. But she turned and smiled at her sister as she walked down to the audience.

Jessica was all by herself on the stage. She felt very surprised that her sister had missed the word.

"The word is *gorilla*," Mrs. Armstrong repeated.

Jessica bit her lip. She tried to remember what Mrs. Otis had told her, "I have to concentrate," she told herself. She remembered the book she had taken out of the library after the class trip to the zoo. She tried to picture the word. "*Gorilla*. G-O-R—" She said slowly. She took a deep breath. "I-L-L-A?"

"That's right," Mrs. Armstrong announced happily. "You are the second-grade winner."

"Really?" Jessica gasped.

Elizabeth stood up and cheered.

CHAPTER 2

The Spelling Star

Jessica looked out at the audience. Everyone was clapping for her and she felt very proud. "I won!" she shouted. She ran down to join Elizabeth and the rest of her class.

"I'm so proud of you, Jessica!" Mrs. Otis said. "I knew you'd do well." She gave Jessica a hug.

"Me, too," Elizabeth said.

"I can't believe I came in first," Jessica said excitedly.

Lila Fowler, Jessica's best friend after Elizabeth, walked over to Jessica. "I thought you'd win best talker, not best speller," she said. Everyone laughed.

"Or best secret-note writer," Ellen Riteman added.

Winston Egbert came up and peered closely at Jessica. "Are you sure you're not Elizabeth?" he asked. "I know you two like to play tricks on us."

"Oh, cut it out!" Elizabeth scolded him, while everyone else laughed.

Jessica shrugged. She was as surprised as everyone else. She had been sure that Elizabeth would win. She felt very lucky to have done so well.

Mrs. Otis's class lined up and began to walk out of the auditorium. The third graders were filing in for their spelling bee.

"Boy, I'm glad it's over," Jessica said. Lila

turned and looked at her. "It's not over," she said. "Don't you know what's next?"

"No, what?" Jessica began to get a nervous feeling in her stomach.

Lila nudged Ellen. "Should we tell her?"

Ellen shook her head. "Not me," she said. "You can tell her."

"What is it?" Jessica begged.

"The winner from each grade at each school goes to a bigger contest," Lila explained in a know-it-all voice. "That means you have to go to another spelling bee. Think of how scary that one will be!"

Elizabeth was walking behind Jessica and Lila. She frowned at Lila. "They're talking about the district spelling bee," she said.

"It's really important," Ellen said.

Jessica felt terrible. She was beginning to

wish she hadn't won. "Another spelling bee?" she muttered. "Mrs. Otis?" she called out to the teacher who was walking ahead. "Do I really have to be in another spelling bee?"

Mrs. Otis turned around. "Yes, Jessica," she said. "It's a very big honor to represent your school at the district spelling bee."

"When is it?" Jessica asked.

"It's in one week," Mrs. Otis answered. "You have plenty of time to prepare."

Jessica's face was suddenly pale. She didn't say anything.

Elizabeth nudged her. "Are you OK?" she asked in a worried voice.

Jessica stared at her sister. She had won because she knew how to spell all the words she had gotten. What if she wasn't so lucky again?

"I don't want to . . ." Jessica started to say.

14

Winston grinned at her. "Don't worry. It'll be like being in the school play. You'll get to be on stage, and lots of people will be looking at you. You'll be the star."

Jessica thought about that for a moment. It *would* be a little like being a star—a spelling star. She always liked being the center of attention. Maybe it wouldn't be so bad, she decided.

"I'll give it a try," Jessica said to Elizabeth. "But I'm going to need lots of help."

"It's a deal," said Elizabeth as she gave Jessica a hug.

CHAPTER 3

Jessica is S-C-A-R-E-D

Elizabeth was doing her math homework before dinner. She was at her desk in the bedroom she shared with Jessica. The door opened and Jessica came in. She sat on her bed and picked up her toy koala bear.

"Hi," Elizabeth said.

Jessica sighed loudly and didn't say anything. She looked worried.

"What's wrong?" Elizabeth asked her. She closed her math book and went to sit on her own bed.

"I'm worried about the spelling bee,"

Jessica said in a shaky voice. "What if I forget everything?"

"You won't," Elizabeth said.

Jessica shook her head. "It was just luck that I knew all the words," she said, hugging her koala tight. "And I only knew *gorilla* because you and Bobby spelled it wrong, and I figured out which way was right."

Elizabeth hated to see her sister so unhappy. She was sure Jessica had won because she was a good speller. She knew her sister could win another spelling bee. All Jessica had to do was practice and try hard and learn not to be scared. Jessica was smart. She just didn't believe she was.

"I know," Jessica said, sitting on the edge of her bed. "You could go instead of me. You should have won anyway—"

"No!" Elizabeth said. "I'm not going in your place. You're the winner."

Jessica looked worried. "But Liz, no one would know it was you instead of me. If you go, our school is sure to win."

"N-O spells *no*!" Elizabeth said firmly. "We'd be tricking people and we can't do it."

Jessica sniffed. "OK, but I'll probably mess up the first word I get."

"No, you won't. You'll be one of the best spellers," Elizabeth said. "I promised I'd help you study. If we work hard, you might even win!"

"Really?" Jessica asked.

Elizabeth smiled. "Yes." She crossed her heart and snapped her fingers twice. That was their special promise signal.

"Girls," they heard their mother call from downstairs. "It's time for dinner."

"Come on, Jess. I'm starving," Elizabeth said.

Jessica gave her a big smile. "Last one down is a rotten egg."

At the dinner table, Jessica told Mr. Wakefield the good news.

"That's terrific, Jessica," Mr. Wakefield said. He leaned over to give Jessica a kiss. "I'm very proud of you."

"We all are," Mrs. Wakefield said.

Elizabeth looked at Jessica and nodded. Across the table, their older brother, Steven, was mashing peas with his fork. "Are you sure it was Jessica and not Elizabeth?" he asked. "I mean, it's pretty weird."

"It is not!" Jessica told him. "I'm smart, too, you know."

"Of course you are," Mrs. Wakefield said. "You're both very smart. I am looking forward to seeing you in the district spelling bee. I'll be very proud of you, no matter what happens. We might even get Grandma and Grandpa Wakefield to come visit that weekend. I know they'd love to see you, too."

Mr. Wakefield smiled at Jessica. "How does it feel to be representing the second grade at Sweet Valley Elementary? It's quite an honor."

"I know," Jessica said. She looked worried again.

Elizabeth looked at her sister. She could tell Jessica's confidence was disappearing. A twin could always tell how the other twin was feeling. And Elizabeth knew Jessica was nervous.

If everyone stopped talking about the big

22

spelling bee, Jessica wouldn't get scared. But Elizabeth had a feeling that everyone would be talking about the spelling bee from now on.

CHAPTER 4

Three Little Bones

Jessica sat in front of the television with a bowl of ice cream. She wasn't really watching the screen though. She was thinking. "Brrr," she said, shivering a little bit.

At dinner, Mr. Wakefield had told her not to get cold feet. That meant she shouldn't be too nervous about the spelling bee. Jessica looked down at her feet. They felt a little cold. She was definitely getting too nervous, and the spelling bee was a whole week away.

She knew her school was depending on her. All her classmates would want her to win. Jessica wasn't at all sure she could. And she didn't want to miss an easy word like *holly* and look stupid in front of everyone.

There had to be a way out of it.

"Jessica!" Steven's voice interrupted Jessica's thoughts. He tossed a paper airplane at her. "I asked you seven times if I can change the channel."

Jessica looked at him in surprise. "What?" she asked.

"You looked like you were in a trance," Steven said. He walked to the television and changed the channel. "I asked you seven times and you didn't even hear me. Are you deaf?"

Jessica's mouth dropped open. "That's it!" she whispered, putting down her ice cream bowl.

"What's it?" Steven asked.

Instead of answering, Jessica jumped off the couch. In the bookcase was their set of children's encyclopedias. Jessica counted through the books with one finger. A-B-C-D-E!" she said excitedly. She pulled the "E" book off the shelf.

"You sure are acting strange," Steven said.

Jessica ignored her brother. She was busy looking for a description of the ear. When she found the section she needed, she sat on the floor to read it through twice.

Jessica read about how sound waves entered the ear and hit the eardrum. The sound waves made the eardrum vibrate, just like a drum. On the other side of the eardrum were three tiny bones. They were called the hammer, the anvil, and the stirrup. When they vibrated, they made the sound waves louder.

"And that's how you hear things," Jessica said to herself.

There was a color diagram of the inside of the ear. Jessica looked at all the details closely. She found all the tiny bones interesting.

"What are you reading?" Steven asked, looking over Jessica's shoulder.

Jessica slammed the book shut. "Oh, nothing," she said, beginning to smile.

She had the perfect plan for getting out of the spelling bee.

CHAPTER 5

What Did You Say?

During recess the next day, Elizabeth saw Jessica talking to Mrs. Otis. It looked like they were having a very serious conversation.

Elizabeth walked across the playground to see what was going on.

"Hi, Liz," Jessica said. "I was just talking to Mrs. Otis."

"Jessica was telling me about her hearing problem," Mrs. Otis said.

Elizabeth's eyes opened wide. "Hearing problem?"

"Yes," Jessica said, staring straight into Elizabeth's eyes. "Remember how my stirrup bone doesn't always work right, so that I sometimes have trouble hearing stuff? *Remember?*"

Jessica was staring so hard at Elizabeth that Elizabeth knew her sister wanted her to go along with the story.

"Jessica, when did this problem begin?" Mrs. Otis asked.

Jessica was still looking at Elizabeth. Elizabeth was surprised that her sister wasn't answering their teacher.

"Jessica?" Mrs. Otis repeated.

Jessica turned her head suddenly. "I'm sorry. I didn't hear you."

If there was one thing that Elizabeth knew, it was that Jessica's hearing was perfectly fine. She was more and more puzzled by the second. She and Jessica had whispered to each other in bed last night, and Jessica had heard every word without a problem.

Mrs. Otis looked concerned. "I asked, how long have you had this trouble? Can you always hear what I say in class?"

"Well, not always," Jessica said with a serious expression.

"Hmm. Maybe I should move you to a seat in the first row," Mrs. Otis said.

"No!" Jessica gasped. "I mean, I can almost *always* hear what you say. I really only have a problem when someone is really far away."

Elizabeth blinked with surprise. She had a feeling she knew exactly what her sister was up to.

"Like when you're on a stage, and someone in the audience asks you something?" Elizabeth suggested.

33

Jessica smiled and nodded. "Right."

"I hope this doesn't mean you can't be in the spelling bee," Mrs. Otis said.

"Oh, no. I wouldn't miss the spelling bee for anything," Jessica said. "But I wanted you to know that I might not hear the words well."

Elizabeth shook her head. Now she understood everything. Since Jessica couldn't find a way to get out of the spelling bee, she had come up with the perfect excuse. If she missed a word, Jessica could always say it was because of her hearing problem.

When Mrs. Otis walked away to remind some boys about the seesaw rules, Elizabeth nudged Jessica.

"Jessica," she said. "I can't believe you said that."

Jessica shrugged and shook her head. "I

had to think of something. I just know I'll goof up on my first turn. I don't want anyone to think I'm dumb."

"YOU ARE NOT DUMB!" Elizabeth shouted.

Some of the kids nearby stopped playing and looked at them. Jessica's face turned pink. "Thanks a lot," she grumbled. "Now everyone's looking at us."

"I'm sorry, Jessica," Elizabeth said. "I just don't think you need to use that silly story."

"I do," Jessica insisted angrily.

"I said I'd help you study," Elizabeth said.

Jessica made a face. "We could study for a million billion years, and it won't make any difference. I still won't do well."

CHAPTER 6

Jessica's Two Tutors

Jessica walked across the playground to join her friends. She kicked a pebble in her path.

"Jessica," Lila called. "Did you start studying for the spelling bee?"

Jessica folded her arms and stood next to her. "No."

"You could still get Elizabeth to go in your place," Lila said. She said it in a teasing voice, but Jessica thought Lila meant it a little bit.

"That's mean," Jessica said.

Lila shrugged her shoulders. "But Elizabeth always gets the best grades in our class."

"It's true," Ellen said. "She does."

"No one would ever know," Winston added. "And that way, our school would win."

Jessica looked around at her friends. Nobody thought she could do a good job in the spelling bee.

She thought they might be right. It made her angry, though, because deep down she knew she was smart.

"Elizabeth won't switch with me," Jessica said. "I already asked her."

Winston put his hands in his pockets. "I could help you study, if you want," he said shyly.

Jessica stared at him. "Why would you want to?"

"Well . . ." Winston looked embarrassed. "When we did the school play and I forgot my lines, you helped me. So I could help you this time."

At first, Jessica thought she should say no. Winston might be playing a trick on her. Then she decided he was trying to be nice.

Maybe if Winston told the others how hard she was studying, they would have more confidence in her.

Jessica smiled at Winston. "Thanks," she said. "I'd love for you to help me study."

On Sunday, Winston came over after lunch. He and Jessica and Elizabeth went out to the backyard and sat on the grass. Elizabeth brought a book of spelling words.

"Spelling is easy," Elizabeth told Jessica. "Say the word to yourself and then just try."

"Yes," Winston added. "Like the word *try*. You say trrryyy. And so you spell it T-R-Y. Easy as pie P-I-E."

Jessica giggled. "Then *you* be in the spelling bee."

"No way!" Winston said. He opened the book. "How about the word *vitamin*?"

"*Vitamin*." Jessica wrinkled up her forehead in concentration. She thought hard about the sound of the word. She said it to herself three times. "Umm, V-I-T-A-M-I-N?"

"Right!" Elizabeth said. "See, you can do it. Try the word *tonsil*."

Jessica laughed. Both she and Elizabeth had had their tonsils taken out. Jessica could still remember how sore her throat was after the operation.

"I can't spell it if I don't have any tonsils," she joked.

40

"Yes, you can," Winston said. "I had my tonsils taken out, and I can spell it."

Jessica stuck her tongue out at him. "T-O-N-S-E-L?"

"It's an I," Elizabeth said. "But anybody could have gotten that wrong."

"You wouldn't," Jessica answered. She frowned and pulled some grass out of the ground.

Winston turned to another page. "Try spelling the word *diary*."

"*Diary*," Jessica repeated. She squeezed her eyes shut. Maybe all this studying would help. If it didn't, at least she could tell people that her stirrup bone was not letting her hear well.

"You can do it," Elizabeth said.

Jessica opened her eyes. "D-A-I-R-Y?"

Elizabeth and Winston looked at each

41

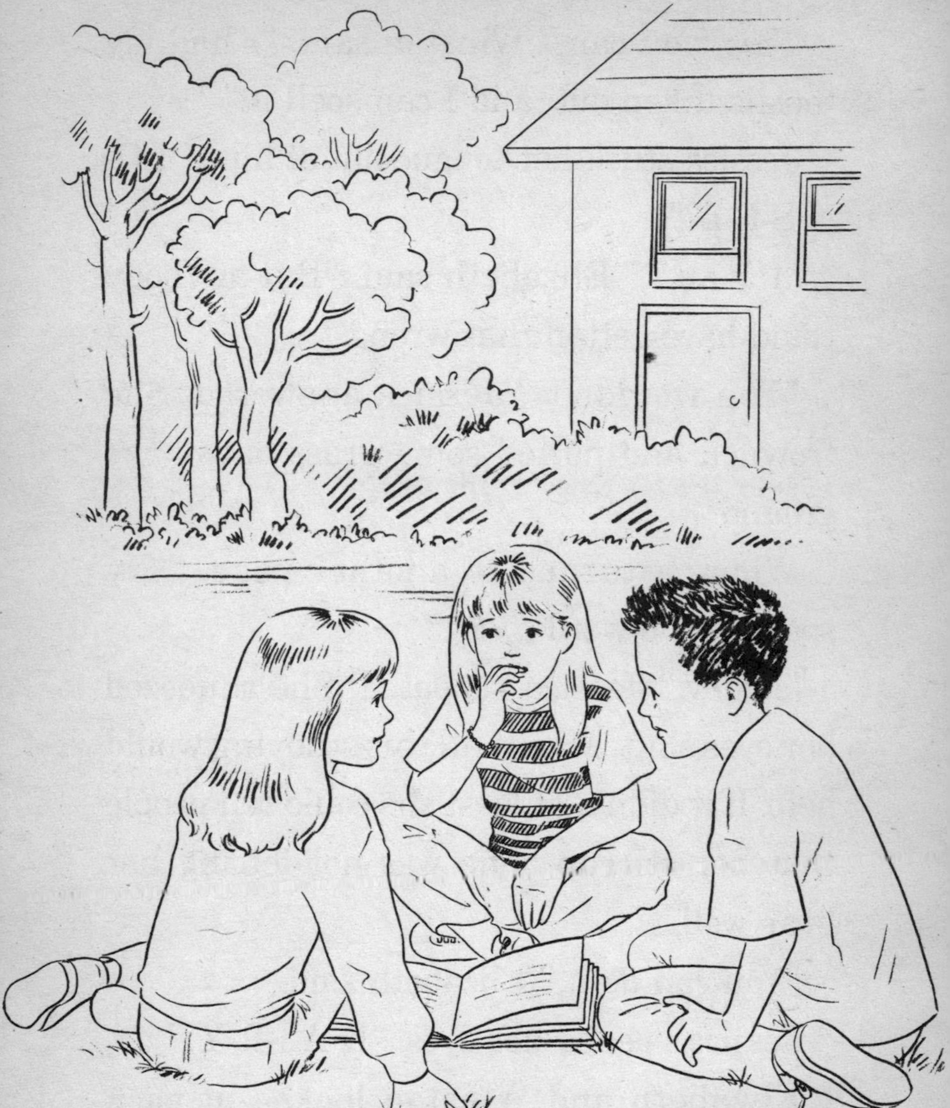

other and then down at the page. "You just spelled the word *dairy*. But it was pretty close," Winston said. They were all silent for a moment.

Jessica gulped. "Liz, you have to go instead of me!" she burst out. "I can't do it!"

"Yes, you can," Elizabeth insisted. "We just started studying. If you say the word to yourself, then you'll know how to spell it right."

Jessica slumped down and put her chin on her hands. She was glad Elizabeth was so confident. She just wished *she* could be confident, too.

CHAPTER 7

The Big Day

Every day during the next week, Elizabeth quizzed Jessica on spelling words. Winston helped out during recess at school. Elizabeth could tell that Jessica was getting better.

Saturday was the day of the district spelling bee. The whole family was going, even Grandma and Grandpa Wakefield. They had to drive in two cars to the high school, where the spelling bee was being held.

"Don't be nervous," Elizabeth whispered to Jessica.

Jessica was busy studying a list of spelling words. She nodded and kept right on reading. Elizabeth decided not to interrupt her sister again.

"I'm going to give you a big kiss for good luck," Grandma said to Jessica as they got out of the car. She kissed Jessica on the cheek. "Just take your time when it's your turn."

Jessica followed her parents inside the school. She had to sign in before the competition began.

Elizabeth saw some of her friends standing by the door.

"Hi, Elizabeth," Eva Simpson said as Elizabeth walked up.

"Hi, everyone," Elizabeth answered.

Most of Mrs. Otis's class was there, including Todd Wilkins, Winston, Lila, Amy Sut-

ton, Eva, and Ken Matthews. Elizabeth was excited about everyone being there.

"Hey, Elizabeth," Ken said. "We were wondering about something."

"What?" she asked.

The kids all looked at one another. They seemed embarrassed.

"Couldn't you go in Jessica's place?" Todd spoke up. "Please?"

Elizabeth stared at him in surprise.

"It's just that we want our school to win the second-grade division," Lila explained.

Elizabeth was so surprised that she didn't know what to say. All their friends thought Jessica would lose. It hurt Elizabeth's feelings.

"No!" she blurted out. "I'm not going in her place!"

"But Jessica isn't as smart as you," Amy said.

"Yes, she is!" Elizabeth said stubbornly. She looked at Winston. "Winston knows she studied hard all week."

Winston looked down at the floor. "She did, but—"

Suddenly, everyone was quiet. They were all looking at someone behind Elizabeth. Elizabeth turned around. Her sister had just walked up to the group. Her face was pink, and she looked angry.

"You all don't think I'm smart, but I am!" Jessica shouted. "I studied all week, and I know a lot of very hard words! Maybe I'll even win the spelling bee."

Elizabeth felt awful. She hated to see Jessica sad and angry.

"Prove it," Lila said. "Can you spell *carbohydrate*?"

Everyone was quiet. All eyes were on Jessica. She took a deep breath.

"Um . . . C-A-R-B-O—" Jessica stopped in the middle of the word. Her face was getting pinker and pinker. Everyone watched her.

"Can you spell the rest?" Winston asked nervously.

Jessica looked like she was about to cry. "I hate you all!" she cried out. She turned and ran back inside.

Everyone turned and looked at Elizabeth. No one could think of anything to say. They knew they couldn't take back what they had said, and they felt terrible.

Everyone filed silently into the auditorium and sat down.

CHAPTER 8

Backstage Nerves

Jessica rushed backstage. A large room behind the stage was filling up with the grade winners from all schools in the district. Jessica felt her heart thumping.

"Jessica, there you are," Mrs. Otis said. She hurried over and patted Jessica on the back. She had a flower pinned to her jacket. "Now, tell me. Is your hearing still bothering you?"

"Well, um . . ." Jessica fidgeted. She wasn't sure what to say.

When she looked up at Mrs. Otis, her

teacher had a kind smile on her face. Jessica had a funny feeling that Mrs. Otis knew that there was nothing wrong with her stirrup bone.

"I think it's getting better," Jessica said softly.

Mrs. Otis smoothed down Jessica's hair. "I know you'll do just fine," she said gently. "And no matter how you do, I'm still very proud that you're representing the second grade from Sweet Valley Elementary School."

"Thanks." Jessica was starting to feel a little bit better. She looked around at the other contestants. Most of them were still studying spelling words. "How many second graders are here?"

"Ten," her teacher said. She pointed out some of the students Jessica would be competing with.

Jessica looked at them carefully. There were boys and girls. She couldn't tell if they were smart or not. She lifted her chin.

"They don't look like geniuses," she told Mrs. Otis.

"No, they don't," Mrs. Otis said with a laugh.

Jessica laughed, too, but inside, she was starting to feel nervous again. She wished Elizabeth could stand next to her onstage.

"Since there isn't a first-grade bee, the second grade competes first," Mrs. Otis said.

Jessica didn't say anything. She just stood as still as a statue and waited for directions.

"Hello, everyone!" called a tall man. "My name is Mr. Lewis. I'd like to welcome you all to the district spelling bee. And I want to wish each and every one of you the best of luck."

"We can't all have good luck," said a tall girl near Jessica. "Lots of us have to have bad luck and lose."

Jessica looked at her with wide eyes. She didn't want any of the bad luck to fall on her. She quickly crossed her fingers behind her back.

"Remember," Mr. Lewis continued. "You are each representing your school. I want to see good manners and good sportsmanship."

"What a lot of pressure," an older boy muttered. "My whole class is here. I hope I don't miss an easy word."

Jessica wished she couldn't hear what the others were saying. Knowing they were all nervous, too, didn't make it any better.

Mr. Lewis looked at a clipboard. "OK, let's have the second graders line up and walk

onto the stage. The first round will start in five minutes."

"Hi, Elizabeth," said an excited voice.

Jessica turned around. Crystal Burton, a third grader from her school, was behind her. "I'm not—" she began.

"I could have guessed you'd win for the second grade," Crystal went on. "I bet you'll win this one, too." She walked away to talk to some other third graders.

"Come on, second graders, let's go," Mr. Lewis said.

Jessica hurried to get in line. Everyone thought Elizabeth was the one who should be in the spelling bee.

Well, she thought to herself, *I'll just show them I can be here, too.*

CHAPTER 9

The Big Bee

Elizabeth held her breath as the second graders walked out onstage. She didn't see Jessica.

"Where is she?" Mrs. Wakefield whispered.

"I don't know," Mr. Wakefield answered. "These are the second-grade contestants, aren't they?"

Steven nudged Elizabeth. "Maybe she decided to back out," he said.

Elizabeth gulped. She was starting to think the same thing. Then she saw Jessica walk onto the stage. Her sister was the very last in line.

"Whew." Elizabeth breathed a sigh of relief.

She could see the rest of their friends sitting nearby in the audience. Everyone was counting on Jessica to win the bee for Sweet Valley Elementary School.

"Welcome to the district spelling bee," Mr. Lewis greeted the audience. "This is going to be an exciting competition. This year we have teachers from Big Mesa, Pinecrest, and Sweet Valley Elementary Schools serving as judges. They will each take turns calling out the words. Before we get started, let's have a big round of applause for all the contestants."

While the audience clapped their hands, Elizabeth kept her eyes on her sister. She could tell that Jessica was still nervous by the way Jessica kept fidgeting and biting her lip.

"Now, I would like to ask the audience for complete silence while the contestants are spelling their words," Mr. Lewis went on. "First speller, please."

A girl with her hair in ponytails walked up to the microphone. She didn't look nervous at all.

"The word is *opposite*," said one of the judges.

Elizabeth looked quickly at Jessica. Opposite was a pretty difficult word. The girl spelled it correctly and went to the end of the line.

Each of the contestants walked up to the microphone and spelled their words. Two contestants were eliminated. In almost no time, it was Jessica's first turn. Elizabeth crossed all of her fingers.

"The word is *cocoa*," the Pinecrest judge said. "*Cocoa*."

Elizabeth shut her eyes. C-O-C-O-A, she spelled silently. She knew Jessica had studied that word. She just hoped Jessica would remember how to spell it. She opened her eyes to watch.

"*Cocoa*. C-O-C—" Jessica began hesitantly. "O—" There was a long pause before she added, "A. *Cocoa*."

"Correct," said the judge.

"Good," Elizabeth whispered. She looked at her mother and smiled. This was exciting.

In the next round, four contestants missed their words. Elizabeth kept her eyes on Jessica. Jessica wasn't fidgeting anymore.

60

Elizabeth hoped that meant Jessica was more confident.

"The word is *barbecue*," the Big Mesa judge said to Jessica.

Jessica stared with huge, round eyes at the judge. Elizabeth felt her stomach do a roller-coaster dive. "Get it right, get it right," she whispered under her breath. "You can do it."

"Can you repeat it?" Jessica asked. Her voice sounded shaky.

"Oh, no!" Elizabeth gasped. Jessica was pretending to have trouble hearing. Did that mean Jessica didn't know how to spell the word?

"*Barbecue*," the judge repeated.

Jessica cleared her throat. "B-A-R-B-E-C-U-E."

There was a sigh of relief from every Sweet

Valley Elementary student when the judge said, "Correct."

Elizabeth sat on the edge of her seat. She was so nervous and excited it was hard to sit still. Jessica was advancing into the next round. "I bet she'll win," she whispered into her mother's ear.

"I think she just might," Mrs. Wakefield whispered back.

Elizabeth squeezed her hands together. She could see their school friends watching Jessica, too. They all looked happy and excited. Elizabeth was glad her sister was showing everybody just how smart she could be.

Elizabeth had always known Jessica was smart. And now everyone else would know it, too.

CHAPTER 10

And the Winner Is . . .

Jessica felt very warm with all the stage lights on her. She was still nervous, but was also enjoying being the center of attention.

Spelling the words seemed to be getting easier. Instead of taking a long time to think now, she was spelling each word right away. Luckily, all the words were ones she had studied with Winston and Elizabeth.

The best part of all was that she had lasted through six rounds. There were only four contestants left, and Jessica was one of them.

Now·no one could say she wasn't smart enough to be in a spelling bee. Jessica knew she wouldn't have to use her silly, made-up excuse about a hearing problem.

"The word is *mosquito*," the Sweet Valley judge said to the girl ahead of Jessica.

Jessica felt worried. She didn't know how to spell mosquito. If the girl ahead of her missed it, Jessica would have to spell it.

"M-O-S-Q-U-I-T-O," spelled the girl.

"Correct," the judge said.

"That was close," Jessica whispered to herself.

Now it was her turn. She walked up to the microphone. When she squinted, she could see her family in the audience. They were all watching her. It made Jessica feel very proud.

"The word is *guitar*," the Big Mesa judge said to Jessica. "G-I—" Just in time, she stopped herself. She remembered there was a silent letter in the word. "G-U-I-T-A-R," she said in a strong voice.

"Correct."

Jessica smiled and got back in line.

"Which one of us is going to mess up?" one of the boys said as she walked up.

"Not me," Jessica said confidently.

The next contestant missed her word, so that Jessica was left with just two others. Jessica suddenly had butterflies in her stomach.

The audience was very quiet. Jessica stood behind the other two contestants, a boy and a girl. The girl went up to the microphone.

"The word is *stirrup*," said the Pinecrest judge.

"Oh!" Jessica gasped. She clapped a hand over her mouth.

"S-T-I-R-U-P," spelled the girl.

Jessica shook her head. She knew it was wrong.

"That is not correct," said the judge.

The girl looked very disappointed as she walked off stage. Jessica held her breath. If the boy ahead of her missed it, too, then she would have to spell it. And she knew *exactly* how to spell stirrup.

"The word is still *stirrup*," said the judge.

The boy waited a few seconds to think. Then he began. "S-T-I-R—"

Jessica squeezed her eyes shut.

"R-A-P," he finished.

"I'm sorry, that's not correct," said the judge.

When the boy walked off, Jessica was all alone on the stage.

"If none of the final contestants spells the

last word correctly, they will return for another word," the judge announced. He looked at Jessica. "But if you spell it correctly, then you are the winner."

Jessica rushed up to the microphone.

"The word is *stirrup*," said the judge for the third time.

Jessica paused. She looked out at the audience. She could see all her friends from school, her family, and Mrs. Otis. Everyone was counting on her. A big smile spread across her face.

"*Stirrup*," she said. "S-T-I-R-R-U-P. *Stirrup*."

"Correct," said the judge.

Suddenly, everyone started to applaud. Jessica waved both hands in the air. Nobody would call her dumb anymore.

Jessica felt like she was walking on a

cloud. She couldn't believe she had wanted to get out of the spelling bee. She felt that this was the happiest day of her life.

"Congratulations," said Mr. Lewis. "You are this year's second-grade winner of the district spelling bee."

Crowds of people came up onto the stage. Everyone started talking at the same time.

But Jessica only heard what Elizabeth said.

"I knew you could do it," her sister told her with a big smile. "I always knew you could."

A few days later, Jessica and Elizabeth decided to do something to celebrate Jessica's spelling victory. After discussing many possibilities, they decided they wanted to have a slumber party.

"Can we have one, Mom?" Elizabeth asked.

Mrs. Wakefield was fixing a salad for dinner. "I think that would be fine. How about a week from Saturday?"

Jessica and Elizabeth both cheered. "How many friends can we invite?" Jessica asked.

"Let's see . . ." their mother made a face. "When I think about how much noise *two* girls can make . . ."

"Mom!" Jessica said.

"How about two friends each," Mrs. Wakefield suggested.

Without wasting a second, Jessica and Elizabeth rushed to the telephone. Elizabeth called Amy and Eva, and Jessica called Lila and Ellen. All of them said they could come.

The twins were in the kitchen discussing the plans with their mother when the back door opened and Mr. Wakefield came in. "Greetings, everyone," he said with a smile.

"Hi, Dad," the twins said at the same time.

Mrs. Wakefield kissed him hello. "You're in a good mood this evening," she said.

"I am," he said. "That's because I'm going on a little business trip. To Seattle. And you're going with me."

"Wow!" Jessica gasped. "Can we go, too?"

Mr. Wakefield shook his head. "No. I'm sorry."

"When is it?" Mrs. Wakefield asked.

"The weekend after this one," he answered.

Elizabeth stopped smiling. "But that's when . . ."

". . . our slumber party is," Jessica finished.

Mr. Wakefield looked confused. "Slumber party?" he asked.

"I just told them they could have one a

week from Saturday," Mrs. Wakefield explained.

Jessica took her mother's hand. "We can still have it, can't we?"

"And who's going to baby-sit for us when you're not here?" Elizabeth asked in a worried voice.

Mrs. Wakefield folded her arms and concentrated. Then she broke into a big smile. "I know just the person. Great-aunt Helen. You met her many years ago, but you were too young to remember. I'll give her a call. I'm sure she'd love to come."

"Why is she called Great-aunt Helen? She sounds very old," Jessica said.

"Well, she's your great-aunt because she's *my* mother's sister. She may not be young anymore," her mother answered, "but she's never been dull. Besides, you'll get to have your slumber party."

Jessica and Elizabeth looked at each other. They were both thinking the same thing. Maybe the slumber party wasn't such a good idea anymore.

Will Great-aunt Helen ruin the slumber party? Find out in Sweet Valley Kids #22, **SWEET VALLEY SLUMBER PARTY.**

SWEET VALLEY KIDS

Jessica and Elizabeth have had lots of adventures in *Sweet Valley High* and *Sweet Valley Twins*...now read about the twins at age seven! You'll love all the fun that comes with being seven—birthday parties, playing dress-up, class projects, putting on puppet shows and plays, losing a tooth, setting up lemonade stands, caring for animals and much more! It's all part of SWEET VALLEY KIDS. Read them all!

☐	SURPRISE! SURPRISE! #1	15758-2	$2.75/$3.25
☐	RUNAWAY HAMSTER #2	15759-0	$2.75/$3.25
☐	THE TWINS' MYSTERY TEACHER # 3	15760-4	$2.75/$3.25
☐	ELIZABETH'S VALENTINE # 4	15761-2	$2.75/$3.25
☐	JESSICA'S CAT TRICK # 5	15768-X	$2.75/$3.25
☐	LILA'S SECRET # 6	15773-6	$2.75/$3.25
☐	JESSICA'S BIG MISTAKE # 7	15799-X	$2.75/$3.25
☐	JESSICA'S ZOO ADVENTURE # 8	15802-3	$2.75/$3.25
☐	ELIZABETH'S SUPER-SELLING LEMONADE #9	15807-4	$2.75/$3.25
☐	THE TWINS AND THE WILD WEST #10	15811-2	$2.75/$3.25
☐	CRYBABY LOIS #11	15818-X	$2.75/$3.25
☐	SWEET VALLEY TRICK OR TREAT #12	15825-2	$2.75/$3.25
☐	STARRING WINSTON EGBERT #13	15836-8	$2.75/$3.25
☐	JESSICA THE BABY-SITTER #14	15838-4	$2.75/$3.25
☐	FEARLESS ELIZABETH #15	15844-9	$2.75/$3.25
☐	JESSICA THE TV STAR #16	15850-3	$2.75/$3.25
☐	THE CASE OF THE SECRET SANTA (SVK Super Snooper #1)	15860-0	$2.95/$3.50